by Michael Sandler

Consultant: Benjamin S. Bucca, Jr.
Head Coach—Women's Tennis
Rutgers University

New York, New York

Credits

Editorial development by Judy Nayer

Cover and title page, ©Reuters/Corbis; Page 4-5 (both photos), ODD ANDERSEN/AFP/Getty Images; 6, Hulton Archive/Getty Images; 7, Joe LeMonnier; 8, Rupert Thorpe/Online USA/Getty Images; 9, Ken Levine /Allsport/ Getty Images; 10, Paul Harris/Online USA/ Getty Images; 11, Online USA/Getty Images; 12, Copyright (C) 1990 by "The New York Times Company." Reprinted by permission.; 13, Allsport UK /Allsport/Getty Images; 14, Getty Images; 15, AP/Wide World Photos; 16, ROBERT SULLIVAN/AFP/Getty Images; 17, AP/Wide World Photos; 18, ODD ANDERSEN/AFP/Getty Images; 19, Manny Millan/Sports Illustrated; 20, Adam Pretty/Getty Images; 21, THOMAS COEX/AFP/Getty Images; 22, Bob Martin/Sports Illustrated; 23, MUSTAFA OZER/AFP/Getty Images; 24-25 (both photos), Bob Martin/Sports Illustrated; 26, Bongarts/Getty Images; 27, ©Leo Mason/ Corbis; 29, Peter Kramer/Getty Images.

Design and production by
Ralph Cosentino

Library of Congress Cataloging-in-Publication Data

Sandler, Michael.
Tennis : victory for Venus Williams / by Michael Sandler.
p. cm. — (Upsets & comebacks)
Includes bibliographical references and index.
ISBN 1-59716-170-5 (library binding) — ISBN 1-59716-196-9 (pbk.)
1. Williams, Venus, 1980—Juvenile literature. 2. Tennis players—United States—Biography—Juvenile literature. 3. African American women tennis players—Biography—Juvenile literature. I. Title. II. Series.

GV994.W49S36 2006
796.352'092—dc22

2005026091

For more information, write to Bearport Publishing Company, Inc., 101 Fifth Avenue, Suite 6R, New York, New York 10003. Printed in the United States of America.

1 2 3 4 5 6 7 8 9 10

Table of Contents

Queen of the Court

As a teenager, Venus Williams had been tennis's shining star. Her **serve** was legendary. It blasted off her racket at 125 miles per hour (201 kph).

Venus's nerves seemed to be made of steel. "This court is mine" was her attitude. Often, she made **opponents** feel like they didn't belong.

In 2005, Venus wasn't at the top of her game. Other players no longer feared her. People whispered that she should quit. Still, Venus believed in herself.

Now, she stood on tennis's most famous court, waiting for her turn to serve. Once Venus had been queen of this court. She wanted to wear the crown again.

In 2005, Venus's opponent, Lindsay Davenport, was the top **ranked** female tennis player in the world.

Wimbledon

Venus was playing at Wimbledon, the oldest and most important tennis **tournament** in the world. The tournament has been played in England for over 100 years. It began in 1877 as a men's tournament. In 1884, a women's tournament was added.

Wimbledon is one of four championship tournaments known as "Grand Slam" events. Winning a Grand Slam event, which also includes the Australian, French, and U.S. Opens, is the goal of every tennis player.

The first international tennis game took place at Wimbledon in 1883.

Players **advance** in the tournament by winning a **match.** Players advance to the championship round by winning a series of matches.

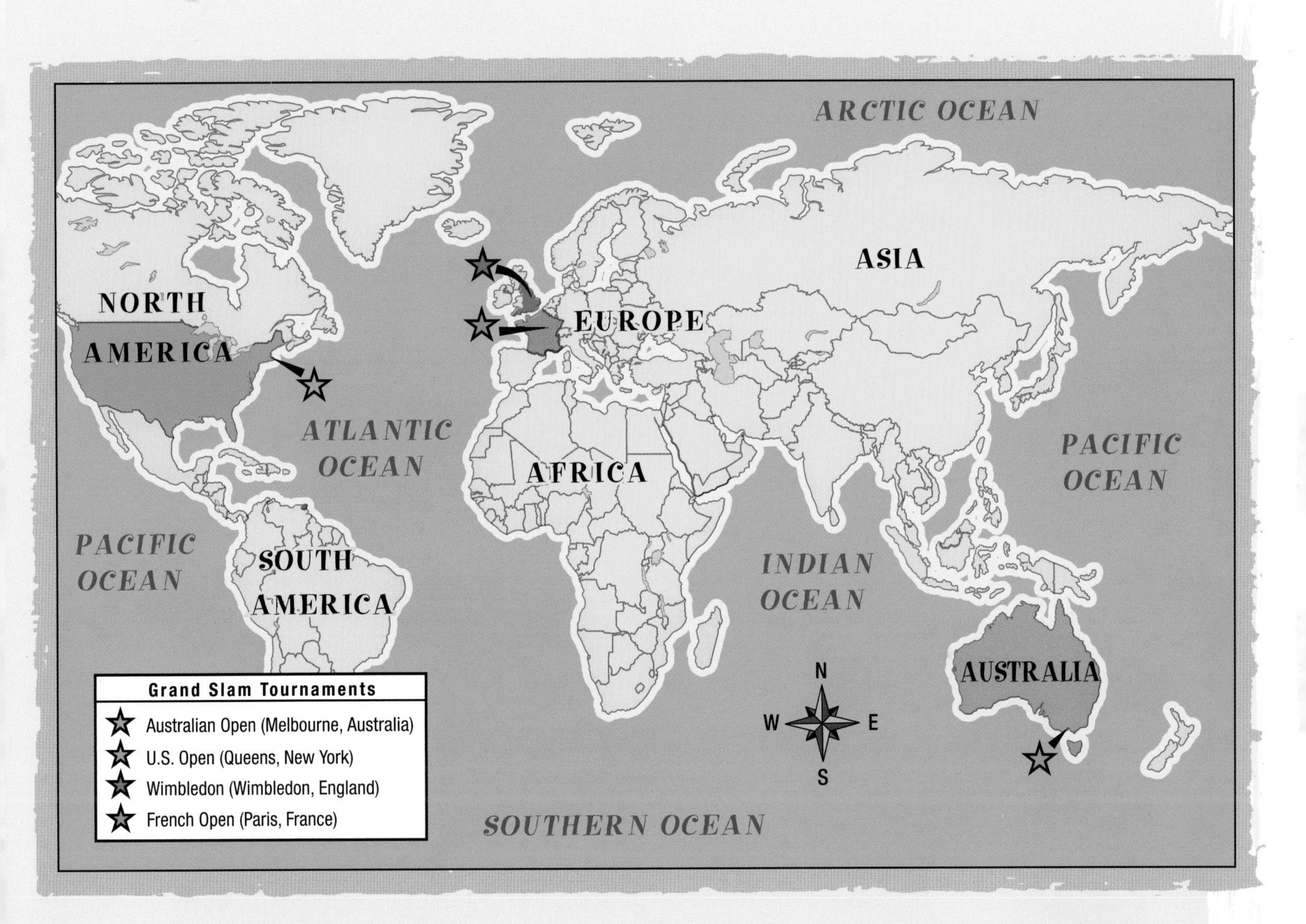

Wimbledon was the world's first organized tennis tournament. Just 200 people watched the first championship. Today, half a million people attend the event.

Unlikely Beginnings

Venus Williams's journey into the tennis world was different from many other players. People think of tennis as a rich person's game. Often, the game is taught at expensive camps and fancy country clubs.

Venus, however, didn't learn to play in a country club. She grew up with four sisters in Compton, California, a tough area of Los Angeles. Many **residents** were poor. Crime was common. Neighborhood buildings were covered with **graffiti**.

The house where Venus grew up

In playgrounds, children listened for the sound of bullets, kept a lookout for gang fights, and tiptoed carefully around pieces of broken glass. Few Compton kids played tennis.

Venus at age ten

Venus's father, Richard, taught his children to duck whenever they heard gunfire.

A Love for Tennis

Richard Williams, however, wanted his daughters to play tennis. When Venus was four years old, Richard filled the family van with tennis balls and rackets and popped Venus into the back. He drove straight to Compton's tennis court.

Richard handed Venus a racket and taught her how to use it. He fed her ball after ball, teaching her how the game was played. Venus loved tennis from the start. When Richard tried to end practice, she would start to cry.

Venus and her dad on the court

Soon, little sister Serena was coming to practices, too. By the time Venus and Serena each entered kindergarten, they both had powerful games.

Serena practices with her dad.

Most parents tell their children not to jump on their beds. Richard encouraged Venus and Serena to do so. He thought it would make their legs stronger for sports.

Making News

The young sisters drew attention for their unusual skills, especially Venus. When Venus was ten years old, newspapers and magazines were writing stories about her.

By this time, Venus was entering **junior** tournaments and was almost always winning. She had everything a great tennis player needed. Her speed let her get to balls all over the court. Her powerful serve frightened opponents.

Status: Undefeated. Future: Rosy. Age: 10.

Special to The New York Times

LOS ANGELES, July 2 — At a time when tennis prodigies seem to be surfacing every week, the latest hot prospect is a 10-year-old Californian, Venus Williams.

Last weekend, Williams captured her 17th singles title in less than a year by winning the age-10-or-under Southern California junior sectional championships.

The tournament, the most prestigious on the California age-group circuit, attracted a record 1,900 entries, with some youngsters forced to play five qualifying matches to reach the main draw.

California and Florida are traditional spawning grounds for national junior champions. The success of Jennifer Capriati, Michael Chang and Andre Agassi has heightened the interest in promising youngsters like Williams, who lost only nine games in her five matches and has yet to be beaten since she began open competition in August 1989.

Michael Tweed for The New York Times

Venus Williams

Matchup With Cheney

Williams, who lives in Compton, turned 10 on June 17. She is ranked No. 1 in the girls' 10-and-under in Southern California, and will move to the 14-and-under division later this month. She already has some of the sport's most respected names talking in superlatives since she beat the legendary Dorothy Cheney in a recent tournament that matched young phenomenons against former champions in their 60's and 70's.

"In the first place, she played like she was 16 years old," said Cheney, who will turn 74 in September and has won 198 national titles. "She looked like she was 14. She was as tall as I am, and I guess she had a size 9 shoe, if you can believe.

"But, oh boy, her game had everything. She was fast, she had a spin serve, she ran to the net, she had forcing ground strokes, her anticipation was good, and her concentration was excellent. Boy, did she wax me!"

The success of the 5-foot-3-inch Williams is not surprising to her father, Richard, a 6-2½ former basketball player who said she was also unbeaten in age-group track meets.

"The most games Venus has lost in a set is two or three," he said in a recent interview. Asked why he had encouraged his five children to pursue tennis, he replied, "I was so flabbergasted at the amount of money paid out to professional players that Mrs. Williams and I thought the best thing we could do for our children is to give them the ability to play tennis."

In an effort to raise money to assist his children in the sport, Williams, who sometimes refers to Venus simply as 'V,' and his wife, Oracene, distributed a booklet to potential sponsors outlining long-range goals. With Venus's success, the booklet has quickly become obsolete.

"A lot of sponsors are standing in line now," he said. "Wilson, Prince, Reebok. They all want to do more for V. Better clothing, more racquets. They call us more. They stop by to see us. Most everyone thinks V will be No. 1 by 1995 or '96."

Williams began teaching his children the sport after subscribing to tennis magazines and buying instructional videotapes.

"I practice Venus and her 8-year-old sister Serena out at East Compton Park," he said. "It's a radical neighborhood. A lot of dope is sold. Somewhere around 70 percent black and the rest Hispanic. The gangs look out for Venus, and they come and talk to her about the mistakes they've made.

"We play on two courts — that's all there is — and they look like trash, they're so slippery. But we will stay here until Venus and Serena want to leave."

Jim Hillman, director of junior player development for Southern California, has seen Williams and is impressed. "She beats everybody," he said. "Kids today think they have to go to Florida to be a tennis player. Their eyes light up at 'room and board.' It doesn't always work. In fact, I can't remember a kid who left us and did anything."

In a sport where first names like Billie Jean, Martina, Chrissie and Steffi have become synonymous with success, Venus sounds like a winner.

"She has all the basic physical requirements to play that special kind of tennis," said Jack Kramer, who watched her last month. "She's very quick, she has a good sense of tactics, and she has a natural service motion. For being 14, she's pretty good."

"She just turned 10," Kramer was reminded. "Oh my gosh," the former great said.

An article about Venus appeared in the July 3, 1990, edition of *The New York Times*

People were often surprised at Venus's talent. They didn't expect a girl from Compton to be good. Sometimes, they made nasty remarks. Venus wasn't bothered by their comments. She knew she was the best.

Venus practices her backhand swing in 1990.

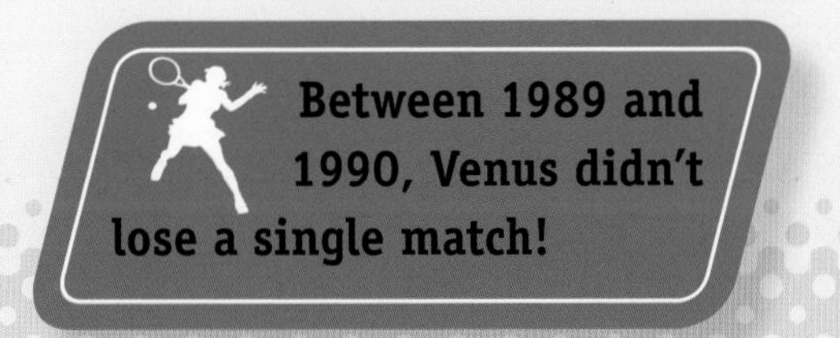

Between 1989 and 1990, Venus didn't lose a single match!

The Next Level

In October 1994, Venus turned **pro**. Tennis fans were curious. They'd read about Venus for years. Just how good was she? Fans quickly learned the answer—she was *very* good! Venus won her first match, wowing the crowd with her **mastery** of the game.

At first, Venus didn't play a lot of tournaments. She was still only 14 years old. Venus's parents made finishing high school—not tennis—her top **priority**.

Venus signs autographs after winning her first match.

By 1997, however, Venus was rocketing up through the rankings. She made it to the finals of a Grand Slam tournament, the U.S. Open. Then, in January 1998, she won her first professional tournament.

Venus reacts happily after scoring a point at the 1998 U.S. Open.

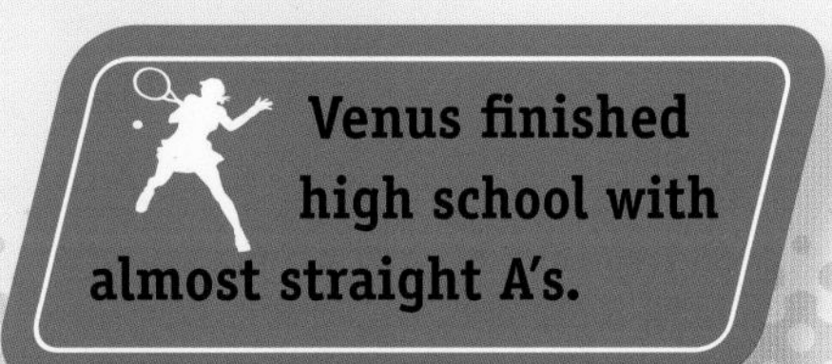

Venus finished high school with almost straight A's.

A Family Affair

By now, Serena had gone pro, too. Surprisingly, she beat Venus in the race to win a Grand Slam tournament, taking the U.S. Open in 1999.

Venus loved her sister, but she wasn't going to let Serena have all the glory. At the 2000 Wimbledon tournament, Venus stole the spotlight back.

Richard Williams, at a match in 1999, cheers on his daughters with a sign that reads "Welcome to the Williams show."

Serena (right) congratulates Venus (left) after their match.

Venus overpowered every player she faced, including Serena! In the finals, she took on Lindsay Davenport, the **defending champion**.

Venus beat Lindsay easily, smacking one impossible-to-return shot after another. She had won Wimbledon, grabbing tennis's most important trophy. Venus had made it to the top of women's tennis!

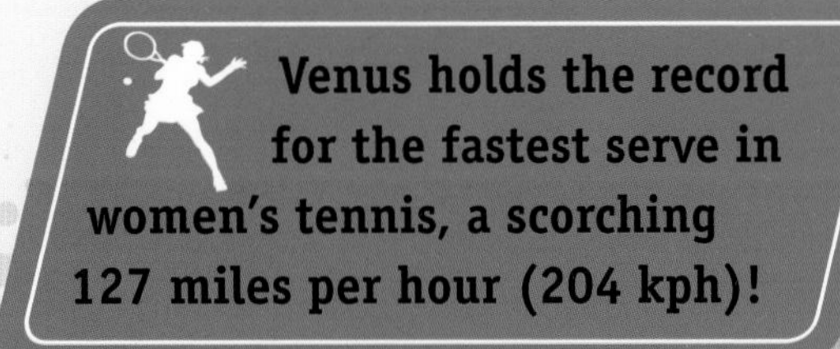

Falling Star?

For two years, Venus **dominated** women's tennis. She won the U.S. Open. She won an Olympic gold medal. Then, suddenly, Venus began losing!

After 2001, she didn't win another Grand Slam event. Winning *any* tournament became difficult! Venus's game seemed to fall apart. Her mighty serve grew weak. She made lots of **unforced errors**.

Players began to whisper: *She's not the same. She's human. You can beat her*. Some people said Venus was burning out. Many players had become stars as teens and then fallen as adults. Everyone wondered if the same thing was happening to Venus.

As Venus struggled, Serena's success grew. She won three straight Grand Slam titles.

In 2002, Venus and Serena became the first pair of sisters in over 100 years to play each other in Wimbledon finals.

A Family Tragedy

Injuries were part of Venus's problem. In one match, Venus tore a stomach muscle. In another, she injured her wrist. Next she hurt her ankle.

However, it wasn't just injuries affecting her game. Venus had a lot on her mind, too. Family came first for the Williams sisters, and the family had suffered a tragedy. In 2003, their oldest sister, Yetunde Price, had been killed in their Compton neighborhood.

Venus limps during a match at the 2002 Australian Open.

Venus had relied on her older sister for support and advice. Losing Yetunde was a terrible blow, particularly when things were already going badly.

Venus talks with a doctor about an injury during a match in 2003.

During one Wimbledon match, Venus had wanted to quit because of an injury. Yetunde convinced her to keep playing. Venus went on to victory.

Return to Wimbledon

Venus never gave up. She rested her body, letting her injuries heal. She tried to get over Yetunde's death, too. Soon things began to turn around. She began playing better. She even won a tournament. Still, to convince those who didn't believe in her, Venus needed to win big.

At Wimbledon 2005, Venus made her way into the championship match. Waiting to play her was an old **rival**, Lindsay Davenport.

Lindsay Davenport in action

Venus celebrates after winning the 2005 Istanbul Cup tournament

Venus's victory over Lindsay at the 2000 Wimbledon tournament had launched her to the top of women's tennis. To return there, she would have to beat Lindsay again. Few believed that she could.

In 2005, Lindsay was ranked number one in the world. Venus wasn't even in the top ten. No player ranked as low as Venus had ever won Wimbledon before.

Battling Back

When the match began, Lindsay seemed ready to win. Her long, flat shots sent Venus scurrying to the corners of the court.

Lindsay won the first **set.** She took the lead in the second. Venus found herself at **match point.** One poor swing of the racket would bring **defeat.** If Venus lost, she knew people would say her career was over. They would say she was all washed up.

Venus **summoned** up her nerve and gripped the racket. Lindsay served the ball. Venus swatted it back. She refused to give Lindsay the winning point.

In women's tennis, a player must win two out of three sets to win the match. A set is won by winning either six games or a **tiebreaker**.

Victory for Venus!

Venus's confidence grew. She felt as if she owned the court again. She slammed balls across the net with power. She placed them perfectly out of Lindsay's reach. She came from behind to tie the match. A third set would decide the championship.

Venus and Lindsay battled on, point after point, **volley** after volley. Neither woman wanted to lose. Neither would give up. After nearly three hours, the crowd rose and cheered as Venus delivered the match-winning point.

"She just took it away from me," said Lindsay. "She was just incredible."

Venus jumped up and down with excitement, relief, and joy. The message in her movements was clear: Venus was back!

The 2005 final between Venus and Lindsay was the longest women's match in Wimbledon history.

Just the Facts

More About Venus and Serena Williams

- ★ **People Named Williams Only**—When Venus and Serena are both playing, there's little room at the top for anyone not named Williams. Since 2000, there's been at least one sister in the Wimbledon final every year.
- ★ **Rivals and Partners**—Venus and Serena don't just play against each other, they play with each other. They've won the Wimbledon title in doubles, where two people play on each side of the court, two different times.
- ★ **To the Stars**—Before she made up her mind to be a tennis star, Venus thought about traveling to the stars. When she was ten years old, Venus considered becoming an astronaut.
- ★ **Making Music**—Venus doesn't just play tennis, she also plays music. Venus relaxes by playing guitar, bass, or piano.

Timeline

This timeline shows some important events in Venus Williams's career.

★ **1980**
Venus is born in Lynwood, California.

★ **1984**
Venus plays tennis for the first time.

★ **1985**
Serena joins Venus at tennis practices.

1980 1985 1990

Venus and Serena play ping-pong on MTV's *TRL*.

1994
Venus enters her first pro tournament and wins her first match.

1995

1997
Venus reaches the finals of the U.S. Open.

1998
Venus graduates from high school and wins her first pro tournament.

2000

2000
Venus defeats Lindsay Davenport for her first Wimbledon victory.

2001
Venus repeats as Wimbledon champion.

2002
Venus loses to Serena in the Wimbledon finals.

2003
Venus loses to Serena in the Wimbledon finals.

2004
Venus fails to reach the finals of any Grand Slam tournament.

2005

2005
Venus beats Lindsay Davenport to take her third Wimbledon title.

Glossary

advance (ad-VANSS) to move forward

defeat (di-FEET) loss

defending champion (di-FEN-ding CHAM-pee-uhn) the athlete who won an event the last time it was held

dominated (DOM-uh-*nay*-tid) had complete control or rule over

graffiti (gruh-FEE-tee) pictures or words made on a building, subway car, or other surface

junior (JOO-nyur) for young people; not for adults

mastery (MASS-tur-ee) having great skill at something

match (MACH) a complete tennis contest made up of sets

match point (MACH POINT) a point that will end the match if the player who is leading wins it

opponents (uh-POH-nuhntz) people one plays against in a sporting event

priority (prye-OR-uh-tee) something that is more important than other things

pro (PROH) professional; an athlete who gets paid to play or competes for prize money

ranked (RANGKT) official position or level; the best player is ranked number one

residents (REZ-uh-duhnss) people who live in a particular place

rival (RYE-vuhl) the main person whom one is competing against

serve (SURV) the shot that begins play for each point in a tennis match

set (SET) part of a tennis match that consists of at least six games

summoned (SUHM-uhnd) gathered; collected

tiebreaker (TYE-bray-kur) a special game played when the score is tied to determine a winner

tournament (TUR-nuh-muhnt) a series of games or contests that result in one player or team being chosen as champion

unforced errors (UHN-forsd ER-urz) poorly hit shots that go out of the court or hit the net

volley (VOL-ee) a shot in which the ball is hit before it bounces on the court

Bibliography

The New York Times

Price, S. L. "Surprise Return." *Sports Illustrated*, July 11, 2005, vol. 103, issue 2, p. 52.

Stewart, Mark. *Venus & Serena Williams: Sisters in Arms.* Brookfield, CT: Millbrook Press (2000).

http://sportsillustrated.cnn.com/tennis/features/williams/timeline/

Read More

Boekhoff, P. M., and Stuart A. Kallen. *Venus Williams.* San Diego, CA: KidHaven Press (2003).

Ditchfield, Christin. *Tennis.* New York: Children's Press (2003).

Donaldson, Madeline. *Venus & Serena Williams.* Minneapolis, MN: Lerner Publishing Group (2003).

Williams, Venus, and Serena Williams. *How to Play Tennis: Discover How to Play the Williams Sisters' Way.* New York: DK Publishing (2004).

Learn More Online

Visit these Web sites to learn more about tennis, Wimbledon, and Venus Williams:

www.backcourt.usta.com/home/default.sps

www.sportsline.com/u/kids/women/williams_sisters.htm

www.venuswilliams.com

www.wimbledon.org/en_GB/about/tour/index.html

Index

About the Author

Michael Sandler, a St. Louis native, lives and writes in Brooklyn, New York. He has written numerous books on sports for children and young adults.